Honey

Dipp

2

Honey Dipp 2
Copyright © 2014 by Reds Johnson
Interior Design Formatting | Strawberry Publications, LLC
Cover Designer | Vassie Thompson, Jr

ISBN-13: 978-1718807266
ISBN-10: 1718807260

Shout out to God!

My mother, Maria and my sister by heart CoCo Amoure!

CHAPTER
One

Mrs. Richardson, can you hear me," yelled one of the EMT's

When she didn't respond, they shocked her again.

"Clear."

"Honey? Honey!"

Honey was unresponsive, but she had a pulse.

"OK, let's go!" one of the EMTs said.

In less than twenty minutes, they were at the hospital admitting Honey.

Guy was torn up. He could not understand what was going on. His heart was literally in pain to know that his soon-to-be wife and the mother of his first child was hurt. Nothing was going to take that pain away until he knew Honey was okay. Not even that.

Just the thought of someone putting their hands on her in that manner pissed Guy off. He didn't know who did it, but he knew the car that he shot at looked very familiar. Just as he was trying to figure everything out, the police walked in.

"Hello, sir. We are detectives Paul and Dan. Can you tell us what happened?"

Guy regained his composure and stood up to greet the police.

"Sir, I really can't tell you anything. When I arrived on the scene, she was alone," Guy said.

He didn't tell them about the car because he wanted to get them first. He didn't want them in jail. He wanted them dead.

"Ok, how did you know that she was in trouble?" Detective Paul asked.

"Honey called me, and I followed her GPS," Guy assured them.

"We will take her phone for evidence," Detective Dan said.

Guy didn't really care about that. He wanted them to leave so he could start his mission. He didn't want to leave Honey, but he had to get this while it was still fresh.

"Mr. Santos, you can see her for a few minutes, then she has to rest," the nurse told him.

Guy excused himself and headed for Honey's room. When he walked in, a tear fell from his eye. She was bruised badly. She had monitors on her belly for the baby. Her eye was black and her arms were bruised. Those were the only bruises that were visible. The rest of them were internal, and Guy prayed for their baby. He took a seat next to Honey's bed and held her hand.

"Baby, I don't know what happened, but I promise you, baby, I will find out. I know you're not with me physically, but I know you hear every word I'm saying. I love you, girl, with every ounce of me, and I promise on my life I'm going to make this right, and you will pull through this and become my wife. I'm here with you every step of the way, no matter how long this takes." Guy gave Honey a kiss on the cheek and walked out.

He fought back the tears that were trying to come out. He couldn't believe this shit happened. He wanted to change places with Honey. He couldn't get the image of her out of his mind. By the time he got outside, the fresh air did him justice. Guy knew he had to get to the bottom of this quickly. The first thing he decided to do was call Vanity. Out of all people, she would probably have an idea of what happened or who did it.

The call went straight to voicemail, but he knew where he could find her. He hopped into his car and pulled off. He could still smell the hospital on his clothes, and he had Honey's blood on the sleeve of his shirt. Guy could not believe this was happening. Everything seemed so unreal to him. He pulled up to Honey and Vanity's store and saw Vanity decorating the window. She spotted him and stopped to greet him. The expression on his face let her know something was wrong. She looked at him with a concern, and he did not wait for her to ask him what happened.

"Honey has been hurt. She's in a temporary coma. I'm assuming it was a group of them. I'm really not sure."

"A group of whom? What coma?" Vanity asked, confused.

The truth was Guy didn't know himself. All he heard was Honey on the phone and the scuffles.

"Vanity, I just want to know if you know anybody that could have done this," Guy said.

He was desperate. Vanity took a minute to think, and then all of a sudden she blurted out, "Unique."

Guy looked up, then straight at her.

"You think ya sister was behind this bullshit? Their beef was a long time ago," Guy reminded her.

"You don't know my sister. I'm telling you I know she is behind this. Who else could do something like this?" Vanity confirmed.

They both knew that Honey could take Unique one-on-one, so they had to figure out who else was with her. Time was ticking, and they were losing. They had to make moves, and they had to make them now.

"Do you think Unique is at the club?" Guy asked.

He was running out of options. Vanity knew Guy didn't want to talk, but she hopped in the car anyway. The ride was quiet. Vanity watched as Guy gripped the steering wheel. She knew he was hurt, knowing how much Honey meant to him. She also knew this meant war, and she was on Honey's side. Honey was the sister she always wanted out of Unique. Unique was trying to live a hood life, but she didn't have the bite to follow her big bark.

When they got to the club, Guy saw the car from yesterday. He knew he recognized it from somewhere — it was Nikko's. A strong feeling of hate came over Guy, but he never mentioned it to Vanity.

They got out of the car and went inside. The club was almost empty, considering it was midday, and that was okay with Guy. Very few witnesses. Vanity spotted Unique at the bar and walked right up to her. Guy made his way to look for Nikko. He knew he couldn't be far.

"Well, look who we have here. What have I done to deserve this pleasure?" Unique said as Vanity walked up.

"Really, Unique? You really don't know how much shit you're into," Vanity said.

"Bitch, do you think I give a fuck. I showed that bitch just who she was fucking with. We laid that bitch out proper. She will know next time who she fucking with," Unique stated.

"Unique, cut the bullshit. You are not anybody around here. If anything, I got more respect than you. Ya simple-minded ass is just jealous, and you don't know how to deal with that. Get ya fucking priorities together and get a fucking clue," Vanity shouted.

Unique was pissed. She couldn't believe the nerve of Vanity, coming at her like this, and snapped. She swung and hit Vanity as hard as she could. The hit didn't even make Vanity stumble. She threw Unique on top of the bar and start whaling on her face.

"Get this bitch off of me!" Unique yelled.

One of the dancers, Strawberry, ran over to break it up. Vanity wasn't going to stop. She dragged Unique by her hair off of the bar and banged her head against the floor.

"Is the sense coming to you now, bitch? Do you have a clue what's going on? You getting ya ass beat like momma should've done a long time ago," Vanity said, still banging and punching on Unique.

The bouncer helped Strawberry break the two apart. Vanity was already on her feet, waiting for Unique to get crazy, preparing herself for round two. Unique finally made it to her feet with blood coming from her mouth.

"You just started a fight that you can't finish," Unique said.

"Bitch, this shit been a war. I'ma show you how to win it."

Vanity spotted Guy coming from the office. He looked disappointed.

"You might as well grab ya shit, cuz we going for a ride," Guy said to Unique.

CHAPTER
Two

Unique didn't give a fuck about anything. She got her ass beat and still thought she was a boss bitch. Everything she tried to accomplish she failed at, and she was jealous of everybody else who made it.

"I'm not telling y'all shit, so this really is a waste of my fuckin' time," Unique said.

She was glad Honey was in the hospital. What tickled her even more was the fact she was in a coma. She wanted street points for this shit.

Guy was getting impatient. In the same token, he wanted Vanity to do most of this work — she was her sister. Vanity walked up and punched Unique out of the chair.

"Bitch, you better start talking or ya ass will be smoke," Vanity said as she walked to Guy's gun case.

Vanity wasn't that type, but enough was enough. She was ready to kill Unique and didn't have any remorse at all.

"Look, why the fuck do y'all care so much? The lil' bitch's mother didn't even give a fuck. She wanted her dead. She got saved because Nikko called the dogs off," Unique said.

Guy was in love. Two more names just came out, but he couldn't believe his ears. Honey's own mother. Guy didn't have a clue she was still around. He really needed to talk to Honey. It was going to be hard finding someone he had never seen before.

Just when he thought all hope was lost, his phone rang.

"Hello," Guy said.

"Hi, Mr. Santos. This is Detective Dan. I wanted to know if you could come to the office before 6:00 p.m."

Guy looked at his watch. It was already 5:30 p.m.

"Yeah, I'm on my way," he said, hanging up.

Time was ticking. He hoped and prayed that the officer could give him more insight than Unique did. Vanity and Guy left Unique tied to the chair. Vanity was not done with her, for damn sure. She wanted Unique to pay just like the rest of them were going to.

They made it to the police station, and Detective Dan was waiting patiently. They went in, and he immediately played the recording. Vanity shed a tear at the sound of Honey's screams. Guy sat there trying to figure out all the voices on the recording. He established with Unique that Nikko and Honey's mother were there, but Guy needed the fourth person. Detective Dan stopped the recording.

"Okay, we have an idea about one of the voices, but we don't have a clue who the others are, and we need your help," the detective said.

"Unique Wilson," Vanity blurted out.

Guy looked at Vanity. He didn't understand why she had said that knowing they had her.

"Who do you know on there?" Guy asked, sitting on the edge of his seat.

"One of the guys is Robert Mason. He's a well-known crackhead on Vermont Avenue," the detective said.

Guy was blown away. Honey's past had caught up with her. The story Honey told him on their trip came through his mind. He couldn't believe this shit. The detective talked for about another five minutes, and then he let them leave. He wanted to find Unique tonight. When they made it to the car, Vanity explained herself.

"I told them about Unique because while they're reaching dead ends trying to find her, we can be looking for the fourth person. Right now Nikko is in the wind, so we need this Robert guy."

Guy knew where this was going. The police were going to make it as a robbery gone wrong. They were not going to believe that this man raped Honey or anything else. They just wanted something to give to the papers.

"Look, I'ma drop you off with ya sister, and you can see what else you can get out of her," Guy said.

Vanity agreed. She knew he was going to look for Robert. She also knew he was going to kill him. Guy's mind was focused. He pulled up to his home and dropped Vanity off. He knew this was going to get crazy, and he had enough respect for Honey to not let one of the people she cared about get hurt. He pulled off and grabbed his .45 from under his seat. He wasn't going to talk about anything. He wanted Robert's head. He could taste the kill on his tongue. In the mist of all Guy's emotions, his phone rang.

"Guy, she's gone. She got away," Vanity said.

"What do you mean *she got away*?" Guy asked.

"I don't know, but when I came upstairs, she was gone," Vanity said.

Guy was pissed as he hung up the phone. Turning the corner to Vermont Avenue, he saw a bunch of fiends. The problem was, he'd never seen Robert Mason before, so he had to be clever not to spook him. He pulled up and parked, then saw Cocoa. She was a well-known crackhead as well, so he knew she probably knew him. He cracked his window when she walked by and got her attention.

"What's up, baby? You need it blown?" Cocoa said.

"Nah, ma, this one's for you," Guy said, handing her twenty dollars. "Tell me, which one of these fellas is Robert Mason?" Guy asked.

Cocoa walked over to the crowd and started talking. All of a sudden he saw Cocoa rub a guy's arm. That was his cue. Guy stepped out of the car with his burner on deck. He kept it out of sight so he wouldn't scare him away and walked with a limp so they would think he was on that shit. As soon as he got close enough, he pulled it out.

Pop! Pop!

The first shot was to the chest, which didn't make him fall. The second was a direct headshot that took his lights out. Guy walked back to his car without a glance back. He heard the screams, but didn't give a fuck. He felt as though Robert deserved everything he got, every inch of that hot lead. In his car, he called the hospital to check on Honey, and there was no change. That made Guy angrier, but also very satisfied that he was making her attackers pay.

CHAPTER
Three

It had been a week since Robert had died. Nikko was still in the wind, and Unique had her time coming. No one knew Honey's mom or where to find her, but that wasn't done either. Honey had come out of her coma, but didn't remember anything that happened to her. Guy was relieved. He didn't want her to remember that day at all. He just wanted her to go on as normal, even though that phone call would be in his mind forever.

Guy sat at the hospital bed with Vanity and Honey. Honey was still in pain internally, but the bruises were gone. They sat there and talked, and Honey was finally smiling again. Guy was happy to see that. Just when they thought things were looking good, Honey caught a sharp pain in her stomach. She grabbed it and yelled out.

"Ahhhhh!"

"Everything okay, babe?" Guy was concerned as he got up.

"Yeah, just caught a slight pain," Honey responded.

It was a little more than slight, but Guy took her word for it. Moments later, another sharp pain came, and this time it was fierce.

"Ahhhhhhhh!" she yelled.

Vanity ran out to get a nurse. Within seconds her room was filled with doctors and nurses. Guy and Vanity were being kicked out so the doctors could work on Honey.

"The baby is in danger. You have to leave so we can do our job," the nurse said.

They went into the waiting room and sat on the edge of their seats. No one was saying anything. Guy was biting his nails. He didn't know what to do. Vanity didn't know how to coach him into believing everything would be okay, but finally the doctor came out, and Guy ran up to him.

"Sir, is everything okay? How's my baby doing?" Guy wanted the answers.

The doctor put his hand on Guy's shoulder and said, "Mr. Santos, the baby is okay."

Guy broke down, but it was tears of joy. He couldn't believe the toll this experience took on him. He was definitely getting the emotional symptoms of Honey's pregnancy. Vanity watched in amazement. Love like this was only seen on television. Suddenly she got distracted when her phone went off.

"She's resting right now, but we will watch her and monitor the baby tonight. Hopefully she will be able to go home tomorrow afternoon," the doctor said.

Guy gave the doctor a firm handshake and took a seat next to Vanity.

"Okay, I got twenty-four hours to find Nikko," Guy said to Vanity as she put her phone away.

"I just got a text from one of the dancers at the club. They said Nikko went to Philly two days ago," Vanity said.

"Is that information accurate?" Guy spat.

"What you want me to do, go to Philly and find out?" Vanity snapped back.

Guy knew he was being an asshole, but he only had twenty-four hours, so he needed no mistakes.

"Nah, that's okay. Look, I need another favor. Honey might be coming home tomorrow, and I'm going to put her in a hotel,

16

she can't go back to that house. I don't need anything else happening to her," Guy said.

Guy wanted Vanity to find them a house. He knew it was a big favor, but Guy didn't have the time because Nikko was his mission. He trusted Vanity. She was Honey's right hand.

They parted ways when they left the hospital and got to work. Guy called one of his friends from Philly. He knew King would know if Nikko was around. King was the boss of Philly, but only standing 5'5" with a bald head, and a scrawny body, people really didn't take him seriously. So, being a light-skinned brother, he must've put in some serious work. King knew what went down, how, when, and why. Nothing went on in Philly without King knowing it. Three rings and King answered.

"Long time no hear from, brah," King said.

He was ready, because he knew Guy didn't call just to chop it up.

"Yeah, I know, but I have some homework that I need help with," Guy said.

He coded everything. The cops weren't on him, but he was from the streets, so he knew the game.

"Okay, tell me the problem and I'll see if I can solve the equation," King said.

"If Nikko left town and came to Philly two days ago without stopping, what time would he arrive in Philly?" Guy said.

"Oh, hell, that's easy. The same day at 3:30 p.m. If I was him, I would book a room at the Four Seasons Hotel," King answered.

Guy caught every word King was throwing. Nikko was hiding in Philly. It didn't matter, because he was gonna die there, too. Guy was heading to Philly. He stopped by the gas station and filled the tank. He handed the gas attendant forty dollars and pulled off.

CHAPTER
Four

Entering Philly, Guy reeked of death. He was hungry for this kill. People who prolonged murder usually got caught, so he wanted Nikko's death to go smooth and quick. Straight off the highway, Guy headed for the Four Seasons Hotel. He did not have a plan, nor did he have the slightest clue how things were going to play out. He just had the image of Honey being in the hospital bed with an IV running through her veins.

To make the scene even worst, she was pregnant with his first child. He clutched the steering wheel tight. Sweat beaded across his forehead. He wasn't nervous, he was angry. No one knew his rage, but Nikko damn sure was going to feel it.

Pulling up to the Four Seasons Hotel, Guy felt his adrenalin rising. He knew what he was about to do could put him away if he got caught, but it was a chance he was willing to take. He parked his car at the corner, still in site of the hotel. Philly was not his area, so he had to peep out the scene. Lurking in his car, Guy's phone went off and surprised him.

"What's up?" Guy said, answering the phone.

"Just making sure you were good. Heard that you touched down," King said into the phone.

Guy didn't know how he did it, but King was the King of Philly. He didn't know how King knew the ins and outs or how he got his spot, but Philly was his.

"Yeah, man, I'm alright. And I found everything I need," Guy answered.

"Alright then," King said and hung up.

Guy got situated in his seat. He knew it was going to be a long night. He waited around until 9:00 p.m., and when he finally saw the time and the person he lurked in the night for, a smile came over Guy's face. Lo and behold, Nikko was in the flesh. A warm feeling came over Guy. He watched as Nikko went into the hotel. Guy got out of his car and walked up to the hotel, but he knew he needed a game plan.

Nikko was on the run, and he was on the run from him, so he knew Nikko was on the lookout. Just as he approached the hotel, he saw a lady walking past as well.

"Excuse me, miss, can you do me a favor? I will pay you," Guy asked.

"Muthafucka, do I look like a prostitute to you?" the woman said.

Guy laughed it off. Back in the day, he would have smacked the shit out of her for coming out her face with some smart shit like that. Instead, he came at her with a different approach. Guy explained to the woman what he needed her to do. He also apologized for any disrespect. The lady agreed to Guy's proposition and took the $250 Guy gave her. She walked into the hotel and Guy stayed a distance behind her. He watched as she walked up to the receptionist and asked for Nikko's room.

"I'm sorry Miss but this guest asked for no visitors," the receptionist said.

"This must be a mistake. See, we just met, so he probably forgot to mention it to you," the lady said.

Guy watched from a distance. He had his fingers crossed, hoping the lady could pull this off.

The receptionist did some typing in the computer and said, "Room 402."

The lady smiled and walked away from the counter. She took the way around to the elevator so it would not look like Guy was with her. They made it to the fourth floor, and this time Guy kept up.

The lady knocked on the door and said "Room service, compliments of the Four Seasons Hotel."

Guy gave Nikko time to look through the peep hole. Once Guy heard the locks turning, he grabbed the lady out of the way and she ran down the hall. When Nikko cracked the door, Guy pushed himself in. Nikko fell on the floor, and his head hit the wall on the way down.

"Now, muthafucka, you must've known I was gonna come for ya ass," Guy said as he drew his gun.

"Yeah, I knew," Nikko said.

Guy motioned for Nikko to stand up, which he did.

"Before I kill you, nigga, I just wanna know why. Did you know she was pregnant?" Guy asked.

"Man, there's rules to the shit. She fucked with mines, so she got fucked, and I don't give a fuck about no damn baby," Nikko said, the words he spoke were cold.

And that was the last thing Nikko could say. Guy went across his face twice with the back of the gun, and Nikko went down again. He grabbed a pillow from the bed and put it on

Nikko's chest. He looked him in the face the whole time he gave him the full clip.

Boc .Boc. Boc. Boc. Boc. Boc.

Nikko's body went limp. As Nikko lay there, motionless, Guy got up and walked out without looking back. Another mission accomplished, but he wasn't finished yet.

CHAPTER
Five

Honey sat up in the bed. "This hotel is beautiful, but I'm tired of sitting in bed."

She was finally out of the hospital, but the doctor still had her on bed rest. Guy explained that Vanity was looking for a house for them because he had too much stuff on his plate at the time. He also explained to her how he didn't want her back to that house, but never told her the truth about why.

"Babe, calm down. Vanity texted me the address to the house, so I'ma go check it out," Guy said.

"So you're going to leave me here by myself?" Honey asked.

"Babe, you're on bed rest, so what do you want me to do?" Guy said.

"I want to get some fresh air. I'm tired of sitting here all day. I'm shocked I don't have bed sores," Honey said.

Guy told Honey that she could come along, and she got up and got dressed. She was still a little weak, but she managed to get ready. He watched her as she got dressed, but her baby bump was adorable. He liked how her belly button started to stick out. She grabbed her coat and they left.

In no time they arrived at the address Vanity had texted, and Honey couldn't believe her eyes. Hell, Guy was shocked himself. It was a beautiful, modern brick mini-mansion. It was gated off with its own security keypad. Guy pulled up and the gates opened. When he got closer to the house, he saw Vanity and a short, white bald-headed guy standing in the doorway. Honey got out, and Vanity greeted her.

"Welcome home, baby girl," Vanity screamed.

Honey gave Vanity a hug. She really missed her a lot.

"Who's house is this?" Honey asked.

"Well, hopefully it will be yours. Come in and let me show you around," Vanity said.

Honey's mouth was wide open as she stepped into the house. Guy stayed behind and talked to the white guy, whose name was Bill.

"So this is 15,000 square feet, which is over six acres of land. It is five bedrooms and two master suites," Bill explained.

"Sounds good. What else is there and how much is we talking about," Guy said as he and Bill started walking around the house.

"Well, it has an in-ground pool, five full bathrooms, and not to mention a gourmet eat-in kitchen with a curved staircase. I almost forgot — there's a full basement with a laundry room and office," Bill finished.

"Everything sounds good and the house is amazing. How much are we talking?" Guy asked for a second time.

"Actually, you're in luck, because it went down for some reason. $250,000 is the asking price," Bill said.

"That's kind of cheap for something so grand. What's the negative side of this house?" Guy wanted to know why it was such a sweet deal.

"Actually, there's no reason, but just to make sure I will double check," Bill said.

"Write up a contract and we can talk," Guy said.

Just as the conversation was over, Honey and Vanity came out of the house. Honey was smiling from ear to ear, but Vanity's face was not a pleasant one.

"Babe, I love this house. It is just what we need to start our family," Honey said.

She gave Guy a kiss when she finally got to him. He kept looking at Vanity. He knew something was up, but he just didn't know what.

"Okay, Bill, you have my number, so hopefully we will be talking sooner than later," Guy said and headed for the car.

When Guy and Honey were in the car, Guy's phone went off. It was a text from Vanity.

Honey's mom is around town asking have anyone seen her. I'm going to keep my ear to the street, but if I find her first the bitch is mine.

Guy knew he only did half the job, but he was ready to finish it. He did not care if it was Honey's mother or not, she was a dead bitch to him.

They pulled off, and Guy was trying to hide his rage, but Honey could sense something was wrong, like always.

"Talk to me, babe. What's going on?" Honey said.

"Nothing, babe. It's nothing to worry ya pretty little head about," Guy said.

They made it back to the hotel safe and sound. Guy sat on the bed while Honey took a shower. With her finally being home, Guy was slightly sidetracked and didn't think too much about Honey's mother. Now reality has settled back in, and Guy knew he had to settle this unfinished business. He didn't know what to do. Even though what happened in the past almost ruined Honey's life, this was still her mother. This put Guy in a fucked-up position. How could he take out her mother? He didn't feel as though it was his place, but he had to think on a plan to put her ass away.

"*Babe!*" Honey screamed.

"What are you yelling for?" Guy said.

"What the hell are you thinking about? I have called you three times while I was standing here," Honey said with attitude.

Guy didn't know he had blanked out. He was thinking too much and never heard Honey. Since she had been pregnant, she had been very aggressive, so the slightest thing, made her want to argue. Guy understood a little, but since this was the first time he'd dealt with this, he just took everything day-by-day.

"My fault, babe. I was thinking about something," Guy said.

Honey put her nostrils down. She was really mean since she had become pregnant, and she knew she just couldn't control her emotions.

"I have a doctor's appointment later, and I'm hungry now," she said.

"Okay, I'll order you some food, and then I have to make a couple errands," Guy told her.

He had to leave because he couldn't figure out anything with Honey in his ear. He called room service and ordered her some food. He gave her a kiss and headed out the door.

CHAPTER
Six

Guy didn't know what to do or who to talk to. He didn't even know her mother's name. He was stuck and didn't know how to come out of it. Just when he thought everything had come to an end and the rest were going to get away with what they did, Vanity came through.

Come see me at the barbershop. I got some info, Vanity texted.

Guy knew Vanity had come through. Whether it was Unique or Honey's mom, Guy didn't care. He just wanted one of their heads on a platter. Unique was not going to get away this time. He didn't have a clue how she escaped last time, but this time he was on point.

Meanwhile, at the hotel, Honey sat on the bed and ate her steak and potatoes. She had really picked up some weight, and she still had five months to go. She didn't care. As long as her baby was healthy, nothing else mattered to her.

When the phone rang, she put the fork down to pick it up.

"Hello," Honey said.

"So, you are here," the voice said.

"Who is this?" Honey asked.

"You don't have to speak, just listen. I don't know what or who your man thinks he is, but he is just making matters worse. What we did to you is nothing compared to what we can do to him," the voice on the phone said.

Honey hung up. She picked up the phone again to call Guy. She did not know what was going on, but she wanted to find out.

"Babe, you have to come back now," Honey said when Guy picked up.

"Honey, what's the matter? Did something happen?" Guy asked.

"Look, just come back now."

Without hesitation, Guy made a U-turn. He knew something was wrong by the way Honey sounded. He couldn't let her get hurt again. That would be something he could not live with. Since he wasn't far from the hotel, he made it there within minutes. Getting out of the car with it still started, Guy ran into the hotel. He made it to the room to see Honey pacing the floor.

"What's wrong, babe," Guy said, giving her a hug.

"I got a call. What's going on? They said something about doing something to you. I don't know what's going on. Tell me what's going on right now. Why would someone want to hurt you?" Honey said.

"Baby, look, I'm going to take care of everything. I don't want you to worry about nothing. Now get back into bed," Guy said.

"*No*! You're going to tell me right now what's been going on. Somebody wants to hurt you, and all you can say is get back to bed?" Honey yelled.

Guy sat on the bed and put his hand on his head. He knew she was not going to stop until he told her, so he just came out with it.

"Look, I didn't want to tell you this. I didn't want you to know and relive your past. Unique, Nikko, your mother and Robert Mason basically beat you, and that's why you were in the hospital. I don't know why they did it, but I promise you that I will handle this."

32

"Why can't I remember?" Honey asked.

"You were in a coma for a week or so. I was glad that you didn't remember. I never wanted you to," Guy said.

Honey put her hand over her face. Her emotions started to run wild. She didn't know what to do or how to feel. Even though she didn't want him to go back to his old ways, she really couldn't be mad at him.

"I killed Robert and Nikko," Guy finished.

Honey looked at Guy as if she had seen a ghost. She couldn't believe what he had just said. The thought of her soon-to-be husband murdering two people was mind blowing. But how could she be mad when he did it for her?

"Thank you," Honey said.

Guy looked up. He couldn't believe her response. He was sure that she was going to be disappointed in him. He stood up and gave her the biggest hug and kiss.

"Listen, I don't know anything about my mother, but if you find her, let me deal with her," Honey said.

Guy agreed. He didn't feel comfortable anyway, harming her mother. Honey lay back on the bed. Guy gave her a kiss and left back out. He had to meet Vanity and see what she had to say.

CHAPTER
Seven

"So, how you want to handle Unique?" Vanity asked.

Vanity informed Guy that she knew where Unique was. She also informed him that Honey's mother was trying to gather up money and put a price on Guy's head. That was something Guy was not worried about. Who really had the balls to take him out? That was actually the last thing on his mind.

"She's a female, so I really didn't want to get involved," Guy said, second-guessing his respect.

"I'm glad you said that, because I think if anyone should to it, it should be me," Vanity said.

Guy looked confused. He didn't understand the beef between the sisters, but it was heavy. For a woman to want to take out her twin sister, it had to be serious. Vanity saw in Guy's face that he wanted an answer, and she gave him one.

"Whether she's my sister or not, Unique needs to have a taste of her own medicine for a change. She needs to be knocked off the imaginary pedestal Nikko put her on," Vanity said.

For some strange reason Guy had a funny feeling in the pit of his stomach. He didn't know why, but something didn't sit well with him. He let it pass and left Vanity at the barbershop.

Heading to the hotel, Guy got a call. It was Bill, the guy selling the house.

"Hello, Bill, glad to see you called," Guy said.

"Yes, I wanted you to know that everything checked out fine. So, you can make a down payment and I will hand you the key," Bill responded.

Guy heart filled with liveliness. He hadn't had that feeling in a long time. It actually felt good for something to go right, after everything had gone so wrong.

"Thank you, thank you. We can meet tomorrow morning around 8:00 a.m.," Guy informed him.

Bill agreed and ended the call. Guy couldn't wait to tell Honey the good news. He knew this would really lift her spirits, and that's all he wanted to do. He made it to the hotel in one piece, and he knew that would make Honey smile. When he got to the room, Honey was sound asleep. Guy kissed her gently on the cheek and after a few moments of tossing and turning, Honey woke up. She smiled at him and wrapped her arms around his neck. Honey still couldn't remember what happened to her that day, but she knew Guy was out in the streets putting in work, so for him to come back to her was a blessing.

"Babe, I have a surprise for you," Guy said.

Honey sat up in bed. She thought Guy had a gift for her. When she saw his hands were empty, she was a little confused.

"Well, where is it?" Honey asked.

"We got the house," Guy replied.

Honey was lost for words. She looked at Guy with her hand over her mouth. She could not believe her ears. Tears ran down her face.

"Guy, don't play with me. Are you serious?" Honey managed to ask.

Guy shook his head *yes*. He knew she was happy, and that warmed his heart.

"So, when can we get out of this hotel?" Honey asked, ready to go.

"We get the keys tomorrow," Guy informed her.

Honey sat on the bed looking dumbfounded. She knew she was clearly blessed, and nothing could steal her joy. Just as they were enjoying the moment, the telephone rang.

"Hello," Guy answered.

"Hey, just the person I was looking for. Honey's mother got ten stacks so far on ya head. Unique will be at the club tonight, so how do you want to play this?" Vanity said.

"I'll meet you there around 9:00," Guy said and hung up.

As soon as he turned around, Honey's eyes locked on his, and she was now standing up. Her facial expression told him just how she was feeling.

"You're not leaving me here again," she said.

She was fed up. Guy was really distant since she came home. She knew he was taking care of business, but to her it just felt like he didn't want to be around because she couldn't do anything.

"Babe, I just explained to you everything that was going on. I need you to stay put. I don't want anything else to happen to you. Not only do I love you, but you are also carrying my child, so you need to relax," Guy said.

"Speaking of the baby, we never made it to my doctor's appointment because you were out handling your business," Honey argued.

Guy completely forgot about Honey's appointment. The best moment in his life was becoming his worst. This was supposed to be a joyful moment, but he was out killing people.

"Babe, I know, and I'm sorry. I know I'm not there for you at the time you need me the most. I just don't want them to come back and finish the job. This situation has to be settled once and for all. Now, either you gonna have my back on this or you're going to continue to act like this," Guy said.

Honey didn't say another word. Guy carried her back to the bed and tucked her in. Once she was settled, he left.

Pulling up to the club, Honey's words still rang in Guy's ears. He waited in the car until Vanity showed up. He had to clear his mind before he approached Unique. He laid his seat back and put his hand on his head. Just as his mind started to roam, Vanity tapped on his window.

"You good, brah?" she said as Guy rolled down the window.

"Yeah, you ready?" Guy said.

"How you wanna do this?" Vanity said.

"I'ma just go and get her ass," Guy said.

Vanity agreed. Guy got out and headed in with Vanity right behind him. Guy felt strange when he walked in, and the club was damn near empty. He wanted to act like nothing was wrong, so he went and took a seat at the bar. Guy couldn't shake the feeling that something bad was gonna happen, and he wasn't gonna be the one to do it.

"Well, who do we have here?" Unique said.

"You know we have unfinished business," Guy said and stood up.

Just as he did, he felt a hit to the back of his head and went down. Guy was dazed, but managed to turn over and see the person standing over him.

"Vanity!"

He couldn't believe it. He tried to shake the hit off, but Unique stomped him down. Within seconds she pulled out a gun and shot it.

Pow!

Not knowing where the shot landed, after the first *pop* Vanity and Unique ran off. Guy's blood poured onto the floor.

CHAPTER
Eight

The next morning was moving day, and Guy was nowhere to be found. Honey had to call Guy's phone over a hundred times, and he didn't answer one time. She sat on the bed in the hotel without a clue of what to do. Tears started to run down her face as, once again, her emotions took control. She didn't like the control that Guy had over her. She realized, just in that moment, without him she had nothing. Finally, she picked up the phone and called Vanity.

"Hey girl, have you seen Guy?" Honey asked.

"I haven't seen him since last night. He never came to the hotel?" Vanity said, trying to sound concerned.

"No, and we are supposed to meet Bill today for the house. Hold on, I have another call," Honey said and clicked over.

"Hello, is this Mrs. Santos?" the voice said.

"May I ask who's calling?" Honey said back.

"Yes, this is Diane. I'm a nurse at Cooper Hospital, and I'm calling on behalf of Guy Santos," she said.

Honey's heart dropped. She started to panic immediately.

"This is Mrs. Santos. What happened?" Honey asked, trying to sound calm.

"Well, he is stable, but he was shot in his chest. Could you please come in so we can talk in person?" Nurse Diane said.

Honey didn't say another word. She hung up the phone and went downstairs to flag down the nearest taxi. Once she was inside, she started to cry again. The baby started to kick like crazy, so she knew she had to calm down.

"Ma'am, are you okay?" the driver asked.

Honey never answered him. She just held her head down and wept softly. The whole ride to Camden, Honey thought about who could have done something like this. No one crossed her mind, but she also didn't know what Guy was into at this point. He was distant and really didn't tell her anything, so she was left in the dark.

Honey knew she had to do the one thing that she hadn't done in a while.

Dear God, if you're listening to me, I just need you to help me right now. Please shed your blessings upon me and cover me with your shield. Protect me from harm. Lord, I just need your love right now. I don't know what else to do, so I'm going to give it all to you. Amen.

CHAPTER
Nine

"Vanity is a snake-ass, ho bitch!" Guy yelled.

"Babe, you have to calm down. Now, you telling me she shot you?" Honey wanted to know.

"No, Unique shot me, but Vanity set me up. This whole time I been a pawn to her," Guy said.

Honey was confused. She didn't understand anything that Guy was putting down. He sat up in his hospital gown with his backside exposed. Honey watched as he tried to get himself together. She didn't bother to help him, because he wouldn't accept it. Guy was a man, and he made sure everyone, including Honey, knew that.

"That skank bitch set me up. I'm telling you, Honey, that bitch shady. I knew I felt funny, man. Yo, man, she hit me in the head with a fucking bottle," Guy said.

"Who hit you? Babe, you're not making any sense to me," Honey said.

"Vanity called me last night and told me Unique was going to be at the club. So I went, but when I got there, no one was there. I sat at the bar, Unique came out and started talking to me and Vanity hit me in the head with a bottle," Guy explained.

Honey couldn't believe it. Of all people, Vanity crossed her. There had to be a reason behind it, but since she was fucking with Guy, the reason didn't matter. Honey was secretly in a rage. She couldn't let Guy see it because he would tell her to calm down because she was pregnant. It was like they had switched roles. Now it was Honey's time to shine. And she was gonna make her mark this time.

"Baby, I want you to calm down and take it easy. The doctor confirmed that you're stable condition but you still do need to watch what you do. You can come home tomorrow, so I'll come pick you up," Honey said.

Guy handed her the keys to his car and lay back in the bed. His blood was boiling so much that it made his stitches bleed.

He knew he had to calm down. He didn't hit women, but he wanted to fuck Vanity up.

Honey knew that the friendship with Vanity was over. It was her and Guy against the world. Leaving the hospital, Honey was on her shit. She was ready to fight or shoot — either one, it really didn't matter. It took 45 minutes to make it to Camden. It only took Honey 25 minutes to get back in town. Turning the corner, she saw Vanity's car parked at their store.

"This bitch really got balls," Honey said to herself.

She pulled up and got out. To her surprise, Unique was in the store. Honey didn't give a fuck. She wanted both of them, so it really didn't matter. The fact that she was in her store is what really pissed her off even more.

"Oh, bitch, really?" Honey said, entering the store.

That was all that could be said. Honey hit Unique with five quick lefts, and Unique was down. She didn't want to make a fuss and mess up her store, so she helped Unique to the car and put her inside. Unique was knocked out and Honey was pregnant, so it took her a little time. From the outside looking in, it looked like a good friend helping her drunk friend, but that was far from what was really happening.

Honey hopped into the driver's side and pulled off.

In no time, Honey was in front of her old house. Unique was starting to come to so Honey hit her with another hard left and knocked Unique out again. She put Unique's arm around her shoulder and dragged her to the garage.

Her adrenaline was running, and Honey was feeling unstoppable. Once in the garage, Honey sat Unique down in the chair and slapped her face to wake her up. Unique moaned and groaned, but finally she came to.

"Get ya shit together, because before you die you gonna answer some shit," Honey said.

Unique straightened up in the chair once she saw a gun pointed at her.

"What the fuck you want?" Unique said.

"I want Vanity. I could give a fuck about you, but I don't," Honey spat.

"Bitch, you ain't caught on yet, but you a college girl. I don't give a fuck about you. You think I would carry beef on for this long. Your mother wants you dead. Vanity pulled that stunt on Guy for the money. I got a pretty penny for leading her to you," Unique explained.

"I haven't seen my mother in years. What does she want me dead for?" Honey asked.

"Oh, girl, you so damn stupid. You are filthy rich and you don't even know," Unique said.

Honey really had no clue what the hell Unique was talking about. She figured the only reason she had anything was because of Guy, so for Unique to say this really messed with her head.

"Your grandmother had a trust fund for you since you were born, and the only way your mother can get it is if you die," Unique said.

Honey had no clue she had other family, let alone a grandmother who actually cared so much about her that she started a trust fund for her.

"Your grandmother supposedly died last month, and ya dumbass been sitting on millions and never knew it. The day we fucked you up was the day you was supposed to go to the reading of the will," Unique finished.

Honey couldn't believe it. Even though she wanted to scream and cry tears of excitement, her focus was on all the trouble these two girls caused. Honey didn't give Unique time to say anything else. She had all she needed to know. She pulled the trigger and let the bullets fly.

Pop, pop, pop, pop, pop.

She hit Unique with five shells of hot lead and watched her body slump over. Honey couldn't believe what she had done. She took someone's life. But in the same token, she didn't regret it. Honey came back to reality and realized she didn't have anywhere to put the body. She couldn't dwell on that now. She had other fish to fry. Going back to her car, Honey left Unique in the garage like yesterday's trash. She pulled off and was on the hunt for Vanity. She thought maybe Vanity would be stupid enough to answer her phone, so she gave it a try.

"Hey girl," Vanity said. She was stupid enough.

"Hey, where you at? I just left the store," Honey said, trying to sound normal.

"I'm still at my house, I got off to a late start today," Vanity answered.

"Ok, well, Amber is on the register, so I'm 'bout to head over," Honey said.

Honey hung up the phone. She didn't know whether Vanity was setting her up or was just as dumb as she sounded, but Honey didn't care. Guy had her back, so she had his. She was determined to finish the fight they started. She got a sharp pain in her stomach, and she could feel the baby kicking. She gave her belly a rub and put her foot on the gas. Honey knew she was at risk, but it was either them or her and her unborn. As she drove, she couldn't keep her mind from roaming about what Unique was telling her. She made a quick detour back to the hotel. She had to settle this before it ate away at her.

She made it back to her room and the first thing she did was grab Guy's laptop. She went to Family Tree and started typing. Honey had her mind set on finding her grandmother, and killing Vanity could wait for a few. She typed non-stop until she found what she was looking for. There it was, a picture of her grandmother, Anita Williams. She was a wealthy widow of her late husband, Daniel Williams, who was a big time lawyer and very valuable to the community.

As Honey read on, she found out her grandmother was now in a fancy nursing home for the elderly. Why would Unique say she was dead? Honey wrote down the address and took off.

CHAPTER
Ten

Honey arrived at the nursing home and sat out front. She didn't know what she was going to say or how her grandmother would respond. She felt as though she had nothing to lose, so she went inside.

"I'm looking for Anita Williams' room," Honey told the receptionist.

"Who might you be?" the receptionist asked.

"Honey Richardson," Honey replied

The receptionist smiled, "She's been waiting on you. Room 219."

Honey took the visitor's pass and walked off. She was really shocked by the receptionist's words. She walked down the hall to the room, and the door was open. She saw a lady with silver hair tied into a bun sitting on the bed. She had on a yellow dress with pink flowers. The lady noticed her, and Honey jumped.

"Oh, my lawd, Honey!" the lady said.

Honey walked over, and the lady stood up and gave Honey the biggest hug she ever had.

"Sit down so we can talk. This is like a dream come true. I never thought I was going to see you again. I told your mother to let you know I was asking about you," the lady said.

"My mother?" Honey asked.

"Yes, child, your mother, Alana. I told her to make sure you came to see me," the lady said.

Wow. Finally, Honey knew her name. For the life of her, Honey could not figure out what her mother's name was. She hadn't heard it for so long, and after her horrid past she didn't care to hear it again.

"I haven't talked to my mother in a long time," Honey said.

"What do you mean?" Anita asked.

Once again, the pregnancy took over her. Honey started to cry and couldn't stop.

"*Miss, my mother is trying to kill me, and I don't know why,*" Honey screamed.

She completely caught her grandmother off guard.

"What are you talking about, Honey?" Anita wanted to know.

"Look, I don't even know who you are. All I know is I woke up in the hospital and my fiancé told me that my mother and her friends beat me up. When I finally caught up to one of them, they said that my grandmother had a trust for me that my mom wanted." Honey was relieved to get everything out.

It really started to overwhelm her. Anita sat there, shocked. She couldn't believe what she was hearing, but she believed Honey.

"Well, child, I'm your grandmother Anita, and why didn't you ever go to your father about this?" Anita said.

"You know my father?" Honey asked.

Anita looked at her in a confused way.

"You mean to tell me that you don't know him?" Anita asked.

"My mother said that my dad died when I was four years old. I left home at a young age because my mom let her boyfriend rape me and didn't do anything about it," Honey explained.

"Honey, your father is alive, and I talk to him almost every day. His name is Jeffrey Richardson. He was a big time lawyer in California, but now he has his own law firm downtown," Anita said.

Honey couldn't believe that all this time her father was alive. For years she believed that her mother was telling her the truth about his death. She realized that her mother had been lying to her all her life, and now she wanted her dead. She let the tears fall freely. She just needed to release. Even though Honey didn't love her mother, it still hurt her because it was her mother.

"Wow, I can't believe it. In one day I find out that I have a grandmother and a father. I can't wait until my baby comes, because he or she will have something I didn't. Grandparents and love," Honey said.

"Oh goodness, you're pregnant?" Anita asked.

"Yes, I am. I'm actually 16 weeks today," Honey told her.

They talked for two hours, and they learned a lot about each other. Honey found out a lot about her mother that she didn't know. She even told her grandmother about Guy, and she wanted her to meet him.

"Okay, Honey, it's getting past visiting hours, but make she you come by and see me tomorrow," Anita said.

"I sure will. I will be up early tomorrow, anyway. I have to start moving. I found a house on Park Drive, 1003," Honey said.

"Yes, you are my granddaughter. I just moved from that house and came here," Anita said.

Honey looked at her in amazement. Immediately she thought about Vanity. It could not have been a coincidence that Vanity picked out that house. This was all started to make sense, but could her grandmother be in danger as well? Honey didn't want to add any more stress than she already had, so she didn't think too much into it. She gave her grandmother a hug and kiss and left.

CHAPTER
Eleven

Vanity was sitting on dough. Her house was amazing. It didn't look like much on the outside, but the inside was beautiful. White carpet, white leather couches. An all-glass china cabinet filled with fine china. Not to mention the winery in her kitchen, which was all marble.

"I see you did some redecorating," Honey said as she walked in.

"Yeah, I'm going to do the yard when it gets warmer," Vanity said.

When she turned around, she saw Honey holding a gun and aiming it right at her.

"What the hell are you doing?" Vanity said.

"The next time you try to call yourself killing somebody make sure they're dead. Guy told me about the little setup, and Unique told me why," Honey said.

Vanity had horror in her face. This was the first time Honey had ever seen Vanity with emotion. Vanity was a tough bitch but right now it look like she was about to crumble.

"Look, Honey, that was business, and I had no clue that Unique was going to shoot him. That's why I ran, because I didn't know how to explain it," Vanity said.

"That is the father of my child and soon to be my husband, and all you can sit here and say is you were scared? You know I was scared earlier when I left the hospital. I was scared of what might happen to me when I came for y'all heads. But after I seen how much damage a little gun can do, I knew I was going to be just fine," Honey explained.

"What are you talking about?" Vanity asked.

"Go ask your sister," Honey said back and unloaded.

Pop. Pop. Pop. Pop.

Vanity's body dropped on her kitchen floor. The entire marble tile was covered in red. Honey stood there with a smoking gun. She let tears fall, because Vanity was like a sister to her. She really loved her. Snapping out of her daze by her phone going off, she saw it was Guy calling her.

"Hey, babe, what's up?" Honey said, leaving Vanity's house.

"Nothing. Ready to get the hell outta here," Guy said.

"You will be alright until tomorrow," Honey said.

Honey was trying to sound calm. After all, she just murdered two people.

"Well, what you been up to?" Guy asked.

"Nothing much, but I want to know what we are going to do about Bill," Honey said.

Guy totally forgot about the house. With everything going on, he forgot about the most important thing.

"Oh, baby, I totally forgot about that. Call him up and meet him with a check," Guy said.

"Ok, I'll do that in the morning. Also, before we hang up, I met someone today, and when you come home I would like you to meet her tomorrow," Honey said.

"Alright, babe. I'ma get some rest, and I want you to try to do the same," Guy said.

They said their *I love you*s and hung up. Honey made it to the hotel and took a shower. She tried to get a good night's sleep, but it was hard due to the fact she murdered two people earlier. She tossed and turned all night. She even woke up in a cold sweat. The baby was kicking her constantly. The sleep was not a good one at all.

The next morning, Honey was dragging. She looked in the mirror and saw she had bags, and when she looked closely she saw a bruise under her eye. Still, she could not remember anything from that night. She couldn't worry about that at this moment, she had to get ready for her doctor's appointment, and she had to meet with Bill.

She arrived at the doctor's on time, as she always did. She was happy because this would be her first ultrasound appointment, and she couldn't wait to see her baby. She was a little disappointed because Guy was not there, but she managed. She went in the back room and lay on the table. The nurse lifted her shirt and put a clear jelly-like substance on her stomach, then rubbed the monitor across. She could see her baby on the screen, and a tear dropped from the corner of her eye. There it was on the screen, a life growing inside of her. It made her feel warm inside, and then she didn't regret what she had done to Unique and Vanity. They could've taken this life from her. Honey knew from that moment that she was gonna protect her child at all costs.

"Ok, Honey, you're all done," the nurse said.

Honey got up and collected all the pictures. She went out front and scheduled her appointment for her next visit and left. On her way out, she called up Bill and scheduled a meeting with him to pass over the check and collect her keys. They agreed to meet at a diner, so that was Honey's next stop. Guy calling brought a smile to Honey's face.

"Hey, babe, what's going on?" Honey sang into the phone.

"Nothing, just waiting for my discharge papers, and also wanting to know why I had to call you first. I'm the one that's laid up, so what's up with you," Guy said.

"Oh, babe, I'm sorry. I had to be at the doctor's first thing this morning, and now I'm on my way to meet Bill about the house," Honey answered.

"Ok, babe. I'ma go and get dress and wait for these papers. Bring ya ass, as soon as you done," Guy told her.

"Ok," Honey replied and hung up.

Honey reached the diner where Bill agreed to meet and saw him already sitting at the table. She walked over and greeted him.

"Well, hello, Mrs. Santos. I almost thought you guys didn't want the house," Bill said.

"Oh, no, we couldn't pass that house up. We just ran into a few stumbling blocks that we had to work out," Honey said.

Honey handed Bill the check and he called to confirm it. This was a lot of money getting handed off at once, so he was just taking precautions. Once the call came in that the check was cleared, Bill handed Honey the keys. Honey noticed that when she reached for the keys, she was shaking.

"I just had too much coffee this morning. I had to have the energy to pack," Honey said.

Honey blew the shaking off. She shook Bill's hand and they parted ways. She left in smiles. Not only was she excited to get the keys to her mansion, but Guy came home today.

CHAPTER
Twelve

Honey was excited that Guy was finally home. Even though it was a very short time, it felt like forever. Honey never wanted to experience that feeling again. The thought of being without him was just unbearable. They were moving into their new home and starting their new life. The movers picked up the last of the couple's belongings and loaded them into the truck. Just as Honey and Guy locked the door of the condo for the last time, the police pulled up.

"Well, we meet again," detective Dan said to Guy as he got out.

Guy walked straight up to him. He was a man first and a coward never.

"Now, what have I done to deserve this pleasure?" Guy joked.

"Well, I'm actually here to see Miss Richardson," detective Dan replied.

Guy didn't think anything of it. He thought they just needed a follow-up report.

"How may I help you?" Honey asked.

"Where were you at 7:30 last night?" detective Dan said getting right to the point.

"I was actually at my store going over the books," Honey responded.

"Ok, what is this about?" Guy butted in.

"Vanity was murdered last night at her home, and with her and Honey being so close, I thought Miss Richardson could help us," detective Dan said.

"No, that's not what you're saying. You're asking where she was, not if she knew anything. Look, if you have anything else to say, you can talk to our lawyer," Guy said.

He went into his back pocket and pulled out his wallet. He handed Detective Dan a card and they walked off. Once inside the car, they watched as Detective Dan pulled off and the movers strapped down their furniture.

"Hold on, babe, I forgot something," Guy said and got out of the car.

He went back to the garage to get his toolbox. He opened the garage door, and the stench was so horrifying that it almost made him throw up. There in the chair sat Unique. All the blood was drained from her body and stained into the floor. Guy couldn't believe his eyes. She was covered with gunshots. He had no time to be shocked or do anything at that very moment so he closed the door and went back to the car.

"You okay, babe?" Honey asked.

"Did you kill Vanity?" Guy got straight to the point.

Honey looked confused. She didn't know why he was interrogating her, but she definitely didn't like it.

"So, I guess I should call you detective Dan now?"

"I found Unique," he revealed.

Honey forgot that Unique was in the garage. She was so focused on everything else that she never moved the body. She got so pissed at herself for slipping up on something so serious.

Guy shook his head, started the car and signaled the movers to go.

"I gotta handle that shit, but until then, let's not make shit too obvious. We gon' go about our day."

The ride to the nursing home was quiet. Honey didn't know what to say, and Guy was lost for words. They parked in the lot and sat for a moment.

"Who are we here to see?" he asked.

"It was a surprise," she said.

"I think I had enough surprises for one day," Guy shot back.

Honey got out of the car with Guy right behind her. Honey spoke to the receptionist and headed for her grandmother's room. Just as Honey had seen her the first time, she was sitting up in her bed. Anita looked over and saw Honey at the doorway. A smile came across her face.

"Hey, grandmom," Honey shouted.

"Hey, baby. What you doing with Pugs?" Anita said.

Honey and Guy looked confused.

"No, grandmom, this is my fiancé. His name is—"

"Guy Santos. I know who he is. He look just like his mother, Shirley," Anita said.

"You know my mother?" Guy asked.

"Like the back of my hand. Now, this is your fiancé, huh? Well, I can accept that if you can accept the fact that her father is married to your mother," Anita said.

Guy and Honey were blown away. They couldn't believe what Anita was saying. Honey found out so much in the past week that her mind was on overload. She was shocked that her unborn was doing well, because she was stressed to the max. Honey and Guy took a seat to listen to Anita's old stories about Honey's parents. She didn't know why they actually split up, but she had a couple of possibilities. Before they knew it, visiting time was over. They gave Anita a warm embrace and headed home.

CHAPTER
Thirteen

Honey and Guy lay on the floor and caught their breath. They hadn't had sex in a while, so really it was over before it started. Honey didn't mind that Guy came so quickly. She was surprised that she still had that effect on him. She was glad he was still attracted to her, considering she had a popped belly.

"When do you want to go see your father?" Guy asked, breaking the silence.

Honey had been thinking about that for a while now, and she didn't know what to do. So many questions were going through her head. She met Guy's mother a bunch of times, but Jeffrey was never there.

"I really don't know, Guy. What am I supposed to say to him? Hell, what are we going to say to your mother?" Honey questioned.

Guy didn't think about his mother at all. He agreed with Honey: what would they say?

"I don't think this is a good idea. It's just going to cause a bunch of confusion," Honey said.

"Babe, you owe it to yourself. Your whole life you thought you were by yourself, but in reality you've had your family beside you this whole time. You need this as closure," Guy explained.

Honey thought about it, and she knew Guy was right.

"Also, I haven't forgotten about Unique and Vanity, either. It will be discussed. I bought us some time by getting my lawyer involved, but sooner or later we will have to deal with this situation," Guy said.

Honey didn't respond. She knew she would have to talk about it. They lay there and held each other until they went to sleep.

They woke up the next morning with boxes all around them. They looked at each other in disgust because the both had the same thought: neither one of them felt like unpacking anything.

"This would be a perfect time to go to my mother's for breakfast and also handle some business," Guy suggested.

Honey knew that Guy wasn't going to give up until she handled this situation. He was going to keep asking her about it, so she just agreed. They got up and showered. After they were dressed, they wasted no time heading out the door. By the time they pulled up, they could smell the bacon from the driveway. Honey got a nervous feeling in her stomach when she saw there were two cars in the driveway. There was no turning back now. She had to go through with it. They got out of the car and Guy grabbed her hand as they walked up the driveway. He knew after this day her life would change drastically. Before they could reach the porch, Guy's mother came outside.

"Well, look at these strangers," she said with a smile on her face.

Guy walked up and gave his mother a kiss on the cheek.

"Hi, Miss Shirley," Honey said.

Shirley rubbed Honey's stomach and gave her a hug.

"I hope y'all bring my grandbaby around more than y'all come around," Shirley said, walking into the house.

Jeffrey was in the kitchen setting the table.

"Come on in and get some hot food in y'all stomachs," Jeffrey said.

Honey looked at Guy, then looked at Jeffrey. It was amazing, because she looked just like him. From the forehead to the chin, they even had the same skin complexion. Honey and Guy took a seat at the table. Home fries, bacon, eggs, French toast, and sausages were placed in front of them. They said their grace and dug in. Every bite felt like heaven to Honey. She had gained twenty pounds already and still had a lot more months to go. Guy decided to break the ice, because he knew that Honey was too scared to do so.

"So, Jeffrey, do you have any kids? Because we can invite them over for y'all breakfasts, too," Guy joked.

"Well, I had three girls, but one died when she was four," Jeffrey said in a sad tone.

"Oh, I'm sorry for your loss," Guy said.

"If you don't mind, how did she pass?" Honey said.

Shirley gave Honey a confused look.

"Well, I'm not sure, actually. I was away when it happened, and when I came back, her mother had moved away," Jeffrey explained.

"Jeffrey, do you know Anita?" Honey blurted.

"Yes, I do, but the one I know is in a nursing home," Jeffrey answered.

"That's my grandmother," Honey said.

Jeffrey dropped his fork and stared at Honey in amazement.

"What is it, Jeffrey?" Shirley asked.

He got up and walked over to Honey. He grabbed her by the hand and stood her up. A smile came over Guy's face as Jeffrey gave Honey the biggest hug he could.

"Jeffrey, what are you doing?" Shirley said.

Jeffrey broke the hug and wiped the tears from his eyes.

"This is my daughter," Jeffrey said.

Honey was smiling from ear to ear. To be accepted without any doubt was the best feeling Honey ever had.

"But wait, you said that you have three daughters. That means that I have sister. Who are they?" Honey asked.

"Vanity and Unique. They're twins," Jeffrey said.

As soon as she heard that, Honey felt sick to her stomach. Guy looked at Honey for some kind of answer, but she gave none. He knew that she was just as shocked as he was. Honey looked at her long-lost father as if she had seen a ghost.

"Vanity and Unique," Honey repeated.

"Babe, let me talk to you for a second," Guy butted in.

Guy knew that Honey was in hot water, and he couldn't let her drown. They went out on the patio, and Honey immediately started pacing.

"Babe, calm down," said Guy.

"How the hell can I calm down at a time like this?" Honey argued back.

She started to become extremely paranoid. How was she going to tell her father that she murdered her sisters?

"Tell me what happened," Guy said.

Honey was hesitant, but she knew that she had to say something.

"After you told me what Vanity did, I went to the store and Unique was there. My emotions took over me," Honey said.

Guy was all ears. He had to know word-for-word in order to help her. Honey explained how she killed Unique and then went on with Vanity.

"So, this whole thing was over money?" Guy asked.

"Guy, my mother wants me dead to inherit my trust that my grandma has for me. Don't you think it's a little odd that the house we moved into belonged to my grandmother, and Vanity picked it out? She was playing us from the start," Honey confirmed.

Guy was overwhelmed. He had to figure out what they were going to do and quick. It was only a matter of time before the cops pieced everything together. They went back into the house and took their seats at the table. Neither one of them was really hungry anymore.

"Is everything okay?" Jeffrey asked.

Guy nodded.

"No, everything is not okay. You just found out you have a daughter that is in a relationship with my son, not to mention the fact that she is now pregnant," Guy's mother said.

"Babe, I know how it looks, but facts are facts," Jeffrey said.

Shirley didn't like the look at all. If it was true, what would people think? Shirley was old school for real. She thought just like everyone else would think: a brother and sister in a relationship.

"Look, we have to go. We have a big day ahead of us," Guy stated.

"Honey, we will have to get together soon. We have a lot of catching up to do," Jeffrey said.

Honey agreed. She wasn't excited at all. She had murdered her sisters. Even though they did what they did, she would have probably second-guessed it if she knew they were her flesh and blood. She and Guy gave their hugs and left.

Guy drove in silence, and Honey had no clue where they were going. At this point, she really didn't care where they were going. She just wanted to get away. They pulled up to their old house, and Honey looked confused.

"What are we doing here?" Honey asked.

"We have a body in the garage. Don't you think we need to get rid of it?" Guy said and got out of the car.

He went to the trunk and grabbed the gasoline container while Honey sat and watched. She watched as he went to the garage and poured gasoline all over it. Her heart pounded, and she knew what was about to happen, but the pregnancy made her emotional times ten. Within seconds, the garage was up in flames with Unique's dead body inside.

He walked back to the car without looking back. The only thing that was on his mind was protecting Honey. The ride home was a silent one, and they both had enough for one day. It was only 4:00 in the afternoon, but with everything going on, they were drained.

CHAPTER
Fourteen

"Oh yes, Guy, fuck this pregnant pussy," Honey moaned as Guy mounted her.

Their sex life was at a standstill with all the commotion in their life, so Guy was enjoying the ride. In and out of Honey's pussy Guy went. He took it slow, because she was pregnant and he didn't want to be the cause of premature labor. Once he felt Honey's warm cream surround his dick, he wasted no time cumin' inside of her. That's the one thing that Guy liked most about Honey being pregnant: he didn't have to pull out.

"Damn, baby. I think since you been pregnant, that pussy has gotten wetter," Guy joked.

All Honey could do was laugh. He always caught her off guard by the things he said. A knock at the door cut off Honey's laughter. They both put on some clothes and Guy, being the man of house, went to go see who was knocking at the door. As Guy opened the door, Honey was coming down the hall. In walked detective Dan.

"What a surprise. What brings you here, again?" Guy asked.

Detective Dan looked completely past him and stared right into Honey's eyes.

"Honey Richardson, you are under arrest for the murder of Vanity Williams. You have the right to remain silent. Anything you say can and will be used against you in the court of law. You have the right to an attorney. If you can't afford one, one will be appointed to you. Do you understand those rights?" detective Dan said as he put the cuffs on Honey.

Honey couldn't believe what was going on. Not only that, Guy was furious.

"Honey, don't say shit, I mean it. I'm calling the lawyer right now. I'ma be right behind you," Guy said, grabbing his keys.

Detective Dan took Honey outside and put her in the car. He took his time with her because of the fact she was pregnant. Guy watched the whole time before he got in his car. He wanted to make sure she didn't get harmed in any way, shape or form.

The whole ride to the police station, Honey felt as though she was dying. Her life was flashing before her eyes, from the time she was stripping to her meeting Guy. Everything was hitting her all at once, and she couldn't control the tears that were coming down her face. The baby started to kick violently. She knew she had to calm down.

Finally, the car stopped, and Honey knew her life was about to come to an end. She knew that if they could prove that she killed Vanity, she was going away for a long time. The thought of her having her baby in prison was just too much for her to bear. She quickly got the image out of her mind. Detective Dan opened the car door and got Honey out of the car. She heard tires screech, and she turned and saw Guy pulling up right behind the cop car. Honey still wasn't relieved. She knew he couldn't hold her hand through this situation. All she could do was remember the words he spoke to her about keeping her mouth closed.

Detective Dan took Honey into a dim room with one square table and two chairs. She knew she was about to get interrogated. Honey took a seat, and detective Dan sat in the other chair.

"So would you like to start?" Detective Dan asked.

"I'll wait for my lawyer, thank you," Honey said.

That is what detective Dan didn't want to hear. He knew a lawyer would just prolong the situation. They didn't have any physical evidence, just assumption and a motive. Honey didn't know that, though she was extremely scared. Guy was on the phone with everyone, and before they knew it, the station was being filled with family, lawyers, and friends. The incident was becoming more than the police thought it was going be. Honey had so many supporters standing around a bystander might have thought they were getting something free.

"Okay, you people have to leave the premises or be locked up for obstruction," one policeman said.

The crowd was getting out of hand. The more the police tried to contain the crowd, the more the crowd was getting out of control. What made the situation even tenser was that there were more people pulling up. The lawyer had finally showed up and managed to squeeze through the crowd and make his was to the interrogation room.

"I'm Robert Simmons, and I will be representing Miss Richardson. What evidence do you have against my client?" the lawyer said.

"Well, we are still gathering our information," detective Dan said.

"Well, contact me when you have everything. Come on, Honey, let's go," Mr. Simmons said.

The detective knew that he had to work fast. He knew Honey was going to lawyer up, but he had to try. Motive was not going to get him a day in court. He had to have full, concrete evidence. He thought that he could shake Honey up a bit, but he didn't think the controversy was going to unfold like this.

CHAPTER
Fifteen

It had been a week since Honey was arrested, and she was still walking on eggshells. She knew it was only a matter of time before they would be after her. Honey wished she could take everything back, but she knew that it was too late. Jeffrey and Guy were putting up all kinds of money to get lawyers involved. They were not going to see Honey fall for nothing. She had too much going for her.

Guy's mother, on the other hand, was not a happy camper. She didn't approve of Jeffrey getting involved due to the fact he just found out that Honey could be his daughter. Guy understood his mother, but at the same time he was upset. She was more worried about her image than helping Honey, who was the love of his life. He felt as though she should have been more supportive, even if she didn't like what was going on. Honey was still pregnant with her first grandchild, and she should have taken that into consideration.

"How are holding up?" Jeffrey said through the phone.

"I'm doing pretty good. Just hate the fact that I've been missing school," Honey replied.

"It will be all over soon. The accusations are ridiculous. I'm sorry for the loss of my child, I really am, but to think that her own sister did it is just downright ridiculous," Jeffrey said.

Honey wished she could tell her father that she didn't do it and mean it, but she couldn't. Her life as she knew it was falling apart. Her relationship was all over the place. And her happiness was turning into sadness by the minute. She talked to Jeffrey a little while longer and then hung up. Just as she did, Guy came into the room.

"Hey, babe, I ran into the one and only detective Dan," Guy said.

That's the last thing Honey wanted to hear.

"He knows a lot, but I believe that someone is feeding him information. Vanity is dead, and he knows things that only she and I know, and we both know the dead can't talk," Guy said.

"What are you talking about?" Honey asked.

"He knew places where me and Vanity met up. He also knew the conversation we had about Unique. Let's just say for him to find out everything he knows; Vanity must have been wearing a wire. I know that's not true, because they would've had more than enough evidence to put us both away," Guy said.

Honey knew exactly who it was. She also knew that she couldn't touch her. Honey was too hot at this point to do anything. One more false move and the dots would connect right back to her.

"Guy, it's my mother," Honey said.

Guy immediately knew that Honey was right. Honey's mother was the only one left to talk. Guy also knew that if she was helping the police, they had her put away somewhere. What was crazy was when this all started, detective Dan had a recording of the people who jumped Honey, and he should've known that Honey's mother was on the tape by her voice. Just then it hit Guy: they were being set up. He knew he had to finish this once and for all.

"Honey, I need you to pack a bag and go to my mother's house for a couple days," Guy said.

"A couple of days? And where the hell will you be?" Honey wanted to know.

"I'm going to make this problem disappear for good," Guy stated.

CHAPTER
Sixteen

Swift as can be, Guy stepped out into the darkness with a black skullcap, black sweat pants, and a matching hoodie. His mission was on, and Honey's mother was the target. Honey was put away, so she was secure. Guy thought about having someone else do the job, but this situation was too personal. He even thought about letting Honey pull the trigger, but this was personal to him. He stressed the fact that Honey was his prize possession, so for someone to continuously disrespect him by fucking with her was personal.

Word was that police had Honey's mom hiding out in an apartment complex only thirty minutes from the county, so Guy didn't waste time making his move. Just around a bend and behind the waterfront was an apartment complex, just like his informant had said. The informant said she was in apartment 302 or 303. They were not sure about that, but what they were sure of was there were two guards and one camera holding the place down. Guy came prepared. He just needed time on his side.

He rolled up slowly. He wanted to make sure he stayed out of sight. One wrong move and his cover would be blown. He got out of the car to take a closer look at the scene. He saw the guard shack and knew it should be an easy task.

He snuck around like a ninja until he spotted the camera. Time was what he really needed. He waited until the camera turned to the other side of the building, and he snuck into the guard shack. With a silencer on his gun, he let off a round, and before the other guard could do anything Guy, slit his throat. Blood was all over the guard shack. It looked like a horror movie.

One thing about Guy was that he always did things in a smooth manner. Unlike Honey, he knew exactly how to not leave any evidence behind. She went off of emotion when she killed, and sometimes that could be messy. Guy put down his weapons and put on a pair of black gloves. He didn't care about ingerprints, it was just the next task. He carefully stuck the sleeve of his shirt inside the gloves right along with his hand.

Guy picked up his weapons and proceeded to exit the guard shack. The place was still quiet. No one expected anything, and that's the way he wanted to keep it. He took a small can of black spray paint out of his pocket and waited for the camera to turn his way. It was a bit high but Guy knew he could reach it. As the camera turned around his way, he stuck his arm out and started to spray the paint all over the lens.

Once that was complete, Honey's mother's death was just ahead. When Guy made it to apartments *302* and *303*, he paused. He looked at each apartment door in curiosity. Apartment *302* had a TV playing loudly, and apartment *303* was silent.

Guy wasn't sure which door to break down first, but something caught his attention. The smell of burning metal filled the air. All Guy could remember were Honey's words, saying her mother was on crack. He knew that apartment *303* was the one.

He grabbed ahold of the knob and twisted it just enough to see if it was open, and to his surprise it was. Guy shook his head as he entered the dark room. Alana had been caught slipping, and it was all because of her using that poison. By the smell of the room, Guy could tell that Alana hadn't cleaned or bathed in days, but that was something he couldn't worry about. Guy could feel her presence as he moved through what he thought was the living room. He stepped on an empty beer can, and that made Alana jump.

"Who is it? Who's there?" she asked.

"The Grim Reaper," Guy responded.

"This is some good shit," Alana said out loud as she put fire to the crack pipe she was smoking on.

When she lit the lighter, Guy appeared in front of her.

"Don't move," Guy warned her.

Alana didn't listen. She quickly reached over and turned on a small lamp beside her. The light was dim and she could only see the little bit of Guy's face that was exposed from under the hoodie.

"Who are you?" she asked in a frantic tone.

Guy smiled.

"I told you, The Grim Reaper," he repeated.

"What do you want?" Alana asked.

"You fucked with someone I love very much, so now you gotta pay the price," Guy explained.

Before Alana could respond, he took out the knife he had killed the second guard with and lodged it in the side of her neck. Blood quickly spilled out of her mouth. That gave Guy a rush, and he repeatedly stabbed the knife in and out of Alana's neck. Alana was fighting for her life as her eyes bulged out of her head. He pulled out a picture of Honey when she was a little girl and put it in front of her.

"Look at it! I want you to remember this face. Remember what that bastard did to her. Remember what you did to her. Now remember what happened to you," Guy spoke in anger.

He pulled the knife out of her neck and shoved the picture back in his pocket.

"Hear no evil," Guy said as he cut off her ears.

"Speak no evil," he said as he cut off Alana's tongue.

"See no evil," was the last thing Guy said before sticking the knife in Alana's eyes and removing her eyeballs.

After everything was said and done, Guy disappeared into the night. He thought about his father and how he had trained him to be the man he was today. Guy was no rookie when it came to killing, but he had put his past behind him. After an hour had passed, Guy was finally at his destination. He got out of the car and put everything in a plastic bag. Guy threw everything in the river in front of him, went to his truck, and changed into the spare outfit. He put his old clothes in a plastic bag and threw them in the river as well. As he got back in his car, it felt like a weight had been lifted off of his shoulders. He could now live in peace.

CHAPTER
Seventeen

The next morning, when Honey woke up, she smelled breakfast. The baby started to kick and she smiled.

"Hmm, I guess someone's hungry," she said as she rubbed her belly.

She got up and headed to the bathroom. After a quick shower, she got dressed and fixed her hair. Throughout the pregnancy, Honey's hair had grown tremendously, and she loved the glow she had. When she finally made it downstairs, the biggest smile spread across her face. There were baby bags all throughout the living room, and breakfast filled the air. Honey entered the kitchen and received a warm welcome from her father.

"Good morning, my beautiful daughter," Jeffery said as he got up and hugged her tightly.

"Good morning, dad. Well, I mean Jeffrey," Honey said nervously.

"No, you got it right the first time," Jeffrey corrected her.

It felt so good to Honey to know that he had just met her, but he welcomed her with open arms.

"Good morning, Shirley," Honey said with a smile.

"Good morning," Shirley responded back dryly.

Honey felt so uncomfortable, and she was getting pretty tired of the disrespect.

"Can I speak to you in private for a second, Shirley," Honey asked as she headed into the living room.

When Shirley came in, Honey got straight to the point.

"Look, I know all of this is a bit shocking and overwhelming at the same time, but I am your husband's daughter, and I am your son's fiancé. All I ask is for a little respect. You don't know how long I've wanted this closure, and now that I finally got it, I refuse to let anyone take that away from me," Honey explained.

Shirley raised her eyebrows at Honey, and Honey folded her arms and stood her ground.

"Well, I do understand where you are coming from, but I have built a foundation that I don't want to be ruined," Shirley told her.

Just then, Guy walked in the house, but as much as Honey wanted to get excited, she didn't.

"You're more worried about your image than you are for your son and your husband," Honey shot back.

"Excuse me?" Shirley said in shock.

Jeffrey walked in because he heard things getting heated.

"Babe, come here," Guy said, trying to ease up the tension.

"No, I have to say this. I was raped by my mother's boyfriend, and after that I was on my own since I was fourteen years old. I worked at diners and fast food restaurants to make a way for myself. After I finally graduated high school, I realized my scholarship wasn't enough to pay for college, so I started stripping. Yeah, I shook my ass for money, but that doesn't define who I am. Your son came to my job one day, and I felt terrible, but he still wanted me, and now he's about to marry me. He doesn't judge me by my past because he knows my story, so if I'm too ghetto or hood for you, then so be it, but I am a part of this family, and you can either accept it or not, but you will respect me," Honey confessed.

Guy grabbed her hand for comfort. He didn't say anythin
to Honey about putting his mother in her place, because sh
needed that. Guy loved his mother to death, but he
judgmental ways bothered him. Jeffrey had tears in his eyes a
he listened to Honey tell her story. He felt awful because h
knew he should've come back sooner. Jeffrey walked over, too
Honey by her hands, and looked her in her eyes.

"Honey, I am so sorry that all of that happened to you.
should've been there. I know I can't change the past and all th
hurt you've been through, but I am here now, and I'm glad Go
reunited us. I want you to know that I will always be there fo
you, no matter what it is that you need. Just know that I, you
father, will always be here for you," Jeffrey explained.

A warm feeling came over Honey, and it felt good to kno
that she actually had family.

"Thank you, dad," Honey told him.

Shirley was still standing there. Honey didn't care for
response because she had done her part. As she was about t
walk back into the kitchen, Shirley stopped her.

"Honey, I apologize, and I am glad that you're here. I hav
a past just like you, and I'm only like this because I neve
wanted to go back to that life. I am proud to say that I have

strong, black woman for a daughter-in-law," Shirley said with a smile.

Honey wiped the tear that had fallen from her face, and she and Shirley embraced each other in a big hug. Guy smiled. He was so glad that his family was now complete. Well, soon to be complete.

"Well, now that we have cleared the air, let's go eat, because I'm starving," Guy chimed in.

Everyone shared a laugh.

"Well, who bought all of this?" Honey asked.

"Me, of course. You know I had to go get a few things for my lil' man," Guy said as he rubbed her belly.

"Guy, how do you know it's a boy?" Honey asked.

"That's how my belly was when I was pregnant with him. His father knew that I was having a boy just a few months in," Shirley said as she smiled from ear to ear.

Honey was excited. Even though she didn't know for sure that she was having a boy, she was still very excited at the thought. They all went into the kitchen and ate breakfast like a family.

***

Guy and Honey were sitting on the couch watching TV. Shirley and Jeffrey had turned down early, so it was just them.

As Honey lay her head on Guy's chest, she thought about the night before.

"Guy, what happened that night?" she asked.

Guy knew that question was coming soon, and he was already prepared to answer it.

"Honey, I love you, and I never thought that any woman would be able to steal my heart, but you have. Just know that your past is now your past, and you don't have to ever worry about the people in it hurting you again," Guy stated seriously.

That was all Honey needed to hear. She knew Guy had handled the situation. A feeling of relief came over her. When she first found out that she had killed her sisters Vanity and Unique, she felt horrible, but deep down inside she had a feeling that they knew they were related. Honey no longer regretted killing them because they didn't have a care in the world about her and her unborn child's wellbeing. They tried to kill her soon-to-be husband, and Honey did what she had to do to protect her family.

Honey Dipp 3
Available Now

CHAPTER
One

Guy sat in the hospital room deep in thought.

"Hear no evil" Guy said as he cut off her ears.

"Speak no evil" He said as he cut off Alana's tongue.

"See no evil" Was the last thing Guy said before sticking the knife in Alana's eyes and removing her eye balls.

Alana's murder kept repeating in Guy's head as he looked at Honey holding his daughter. He dared anyone to cross his path trying to harm them two, and he was going to make sure they would suffer the consequences. He never knew he could love anyone so much until he met Honey, and until he laid eyes on his daughter.

"She looks just like you" Honey said with a smile.

"Yea she gone be a heartbreaker like her daddy" Guy joked.

"Oh hush up. So we bought so many boy clothes thinking we were having a boy, and she fooled us. Now we have to go shopping again" Honey stated.

"Don't you worry about none of that beautiful. I'll handle everything" Guy assured her.

Honey smiled. She loved how Guy made sure everything was taken care of. She literally wanted for nothing, and she knew that he was going to spoil Mi'Joy. Guy could tell that Honey was tired so he took the baby so she could get some rest. He still couldn't believe that he was a father. It was all so unreal to him. He knew his mother was going to be upset because he didn't call her, but he wanted Honey to be as comfortable as possible. Guy knew that his mother could be a bitch when she wanted to, and he didn't want his daughter being around the negativity. At this very moment Guy wished that his father was there to see his accomplishments. He knew that he would be proud unlike his mother. Guy loved his mother to death, but her stuck up ways turned him off. She was always so worried about her image. What made Guy so upset was that his father brought his mother out of the slums so when she threw shade towards people who came out of the hood bothered him. Guy was so wrapped up in his thoughts that he didn't realize the nurse had walked in.

"Hello Mr. Santos, I just wanted to see how Honey was doing" said the nurse.

"Oh she's fine. I suggested that she get some rest" Guy responded.

"Yes right now that is the best thing to do. Her delivery was a success considering she is a first time mother she did very good. Now we will have her on some pain medicine once she is released which will be on Monday" the nurse explained.

Guy nodded his head as she spoke. He figured since today was Friday and Honey wouldn't get out of the hospital until Monday that he should call his mother, and Jeffrey. He was glad that Jeffrey would be able to build a relationship with his daughter and granddaughter.

End of Excerpt

Reds Johnson also known as Anne Marie, is a twenty-three-year-old independent author born and raised in New Jersey. She started writing at the age of nine years old, and ever since then, writing has been her passion. Her inspirations were Danielle Santiago, and Wahida Clark. Once she came across their books; Reds pushed to get discovered around the age of thirteen going on fourteen.

To be such a young woman, the stories she wrote hit so close to home for many. She writes urban, romance, erotica, bbw, and teen stories and each book she penned is based on true events; whether she's been through it or witnessed it. After being homeless and watching her mother struggle for many years, Reds knew that it was time to strive harder. Her passion seeped through her pores so she knew that it was only a matter of time before someone gave her a chance.

Leaping head first into the industry and making more than a few mistakes; Reds now has the ability to take control of her writing career. She is on a new path to success and is aiming for bigger and better opportunities.

Visit my website www.iamredsjohnson.com

MORE TITLES BY REDS JOHNSON

SILVER PLATTER HOE 6 BOOK SERIES

HARMONY & CHAOS 6 BOOK SERIES

MORE TITLES BY REDS JOHNSON

NEVER TRUST A RATCHET BITCH 3 BOOK SERIES

TEEN BOOKS

A PROSTITUTE'S CONFESSIONS SERIES

CLOSED LEGS DON'T GET FED SERIES

MORE TITLES BY REDS JOHNSON

OTHER TITLES BY REDS JOHNSON

Made in the USA
Coppell, TX
19 August 2021